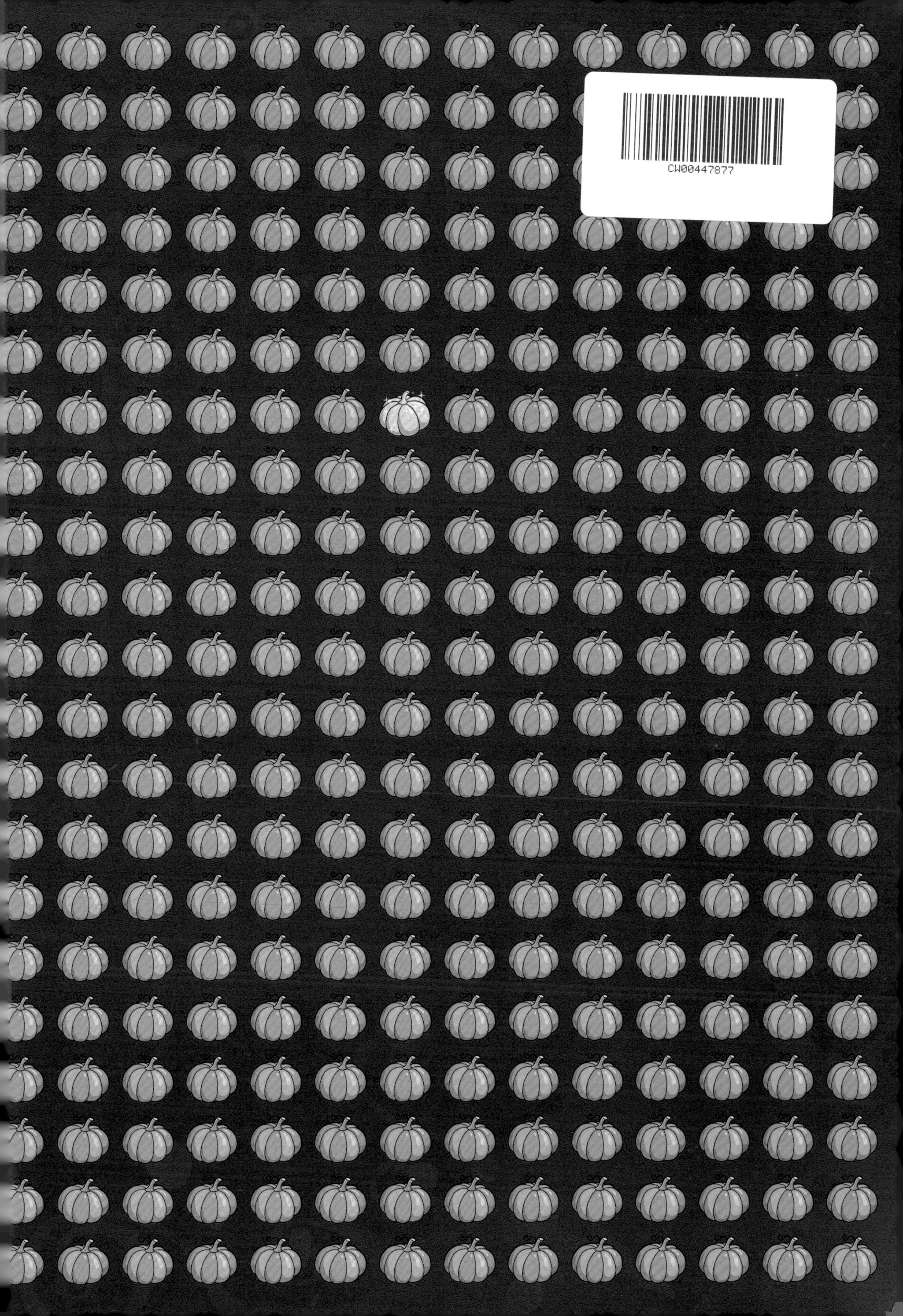
CW00447877

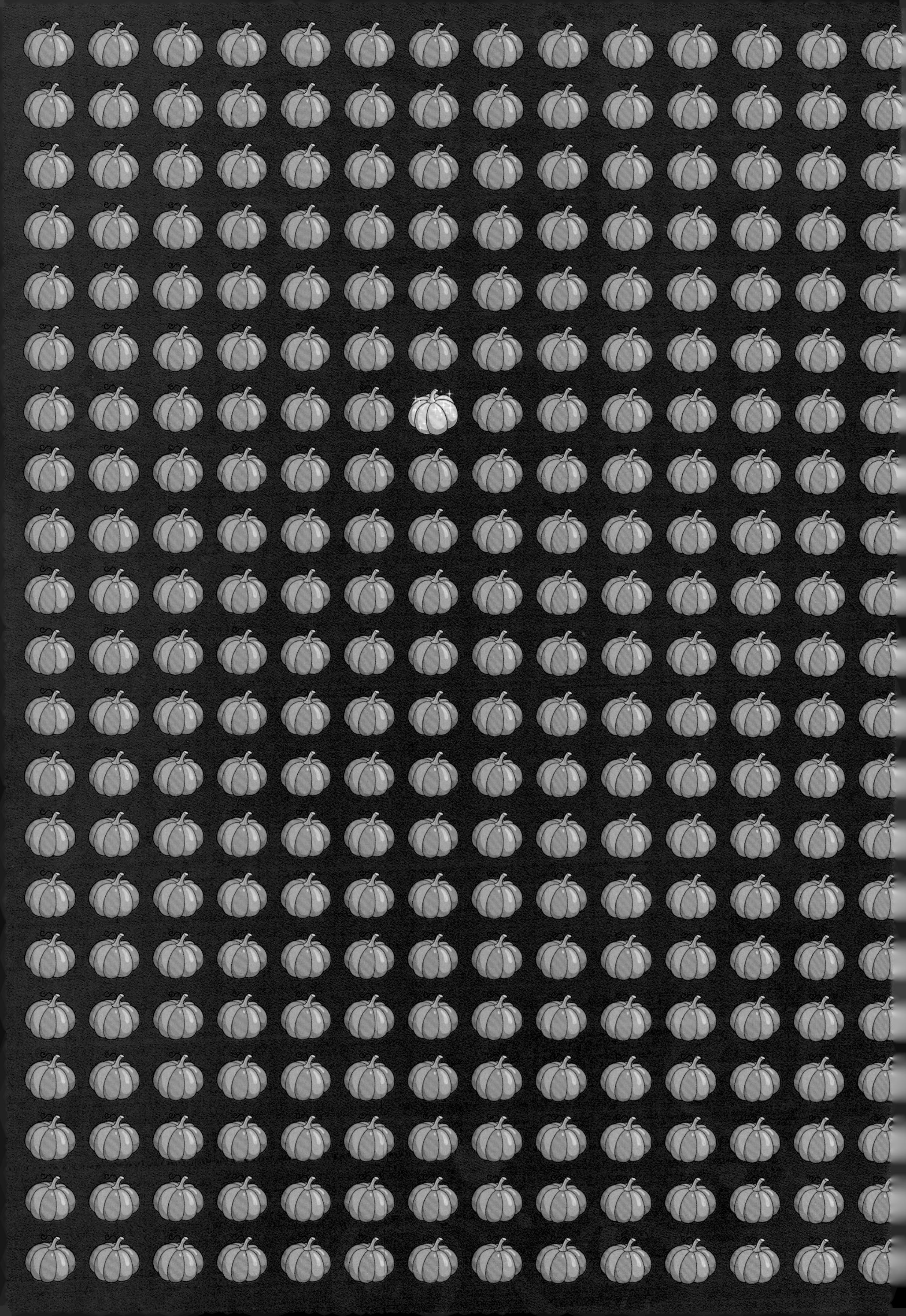

WHERE'S THE PUMPKIN?

SCHOLASTIC

LET THE
SEARCH BEGIN!

Castle Gloombog is home to a strange assortment of scary creatures. Its grounds are traipsed by trolls, its halls haunted by howling werewolves and its towers topped with fearsome gargoyles.

It's the eve of Castle Gloombog's annual Halloween party, and the creatures are putting the finishing touches to an impressive pumpkin pyramid when witch Harriet the Hairy tries to hurry things along with a spell... Only it goes spectacularly wrong! Her magic backfires, making a mountain of over one hundred magical pumpkins vanish!

Now, the spooky squad must trade in their dingy dungeons for the city sights of our world, travelling through time and space, on a hunt to get their precious pumpkins back in time for the party.

CAN YOU HELP THEM?

There are **NINE** orange pumpkins to spot in each scene, along with **ONE** magical golden pumpkin.

ORANGE PUMPKIN

MAGICAL GOLDEN PUMPKIN

Ready to get started on a spooky search-and-find adventure?

SPOOKY SQUAD

This scary bunch are on a mission to find the missing pumpkins. Keep an eye out for them in every scene – they'll do their best to blend in!

Harriet the Hairy

Excitable Harriet loves to dream up brand-new, spectacular spells. The trouble is, her enthusiasm often outweighs her talent and she ends up creating a whole heap of chaos...

Likes: toads
Dislikes: bubble baths

Tangle the Tiny

Tangle, the most colossal spider to ever scuttle the corridors of Castle Gloombog, has a nasty habit of hiding in the shadows to listen in on private conversations.

Likes: juicy secrets
Dislikes: vacuum cleaners

Dorian the Dismal

Over one thousand years old at his last count, Dorian spends his days sighing, staring wistfully out of windows, and remembering the good old days before sliced bread.

Likes: sad violin music
Dislikes: laughter

Liesel the Lumpy

Proud to adorn the loftiest spire of Castle Gloombog, Liesel entertains herself by counting ravens and shouting insults at passers-by.

Likes: beautiful sunsets
Dislikes: bird poop

Dave the Dramatic

Where there's drama, there's Dave. This skeleton likes nothing more than stirring the pot and being at the centre of any fuss or commotion in the castle.

Likes: invading people's personal space

Dislikes: missing parties

Grurg the Growler

Fierce or friendly, it's hard to tell when it comes to Grurg, who only speaks the ancient language of Trollish. He's Castle Gloombog's oldest resident, and keeps himself to himself.

Likes: dark, dank places

Dislikes: early bedtimes

Mutt the Murderous

With a bite way worse than his bark, it's a good job that playful Mutt would rather chase his own tail than hunt down a human.

Likes: fetching big sticks

Dislikes: full moons

Viola the Vague

Despite floating around its halls for hundreds of years, Viola is always getting lost in the castle. She once got stuck wafting around the maze-like library for a whole week.

Likes: open spaces

Dislikes: remembering directions

Frankie the Fragile

Frankie's creator was in a bit of a rush the day he put her together. Still, what she lacks in working body parts, she more than makes up for with her creative thinking and sunny personality.

Likes: colour by numbers

Dislikes: loud noises

THE GRAND CANAL • VENICE • ITALY

MENACING VENICE

Witch Harriet has whisked the spooky squad to one of the places the pumpkins might have ended up. For once, her spell has worked just the way it should! The creatures are capering around the Italian city of Venice, searching for them.

The sunlight is sizzling vampire Dorian's marble skin and Grurg the troll is thinking of slinking off to hide under one of the city's many bridges. Can you help the creatures find all ten pumpkins before one sinks to the bottom of a canal with a *SPLASH*?

LOST IN THE LOUVRE
Next, it's off to Paris – city of love, light and ... pumpkins! Outside the Louvre art gallery, the monsters are on a mission to gather up ten more of the missing Halloween decorations.
Liesel's sneaking off to nearby Notre Dame Cathedral to catch up with some long-lost gargoyle relatives. As the crowd jostles around her, Frankie's just trying to hang on to all her arms and legs.
Who else can you spot in the scene?

THE LOUVRE • PARIS • FRANCE

PARK GÜELL • BARCELONA • SPAIN

RK PUMPKINS
In this s dish park, high above the city
of Barc spooky squad are continuing
their sea colourful ture is
cry from dingy ar vers
their ho, Castl
Harriet's trying to keep everyone together, but
the winding staircases and wiggly paths have
got Viola the ghost all turned around. And now
Mutt the werewolf's zooming off to look for some
canine friends to play fetch with. The group will
never find all the pumpkins at this rate!

TRAFALGAR SQUARE • LONDON • ENGLAND

SCARE IN THE SQUARE
It's a grey day in Trafalgar Square, London, but maybe that will make it easier to spot a flash of pumpkin orange! Harriet hopes it's not going to rain – witches hate getting wet!
Dave the skeleton has slunk off to do a spot of people watching while Tangle the spider is scuttling over to a fountain, hoping to toss in a sparkling coin and make a wish. Is there a sparkling golden pumpkin somewhere, too?

CREEPY CAUSEWAY
Legend has it that this dramatic landscape in Northern Ireland was created by giants! There are none here today, but there is a giant spider, along with a troll, a werewolf, a vampire and more...
The pumpkins are hidden somewhere in the scene and it's up to Harriet and the others to find them. There's not long until the Halloween party is supposed to start, so help them scoop up those pumpkins, sharpish!

GIANT'S CAUSEWAY • COUNTY ANTRIM • NORTHERN IRELAND

BERGEN • NORWAY

MOUNTAIN MONSTERS
The people of Bergen have seen it all – fierce snowstorms, raging seas and now, frantic monsters! The creatures are searching the steep streets for any sign of the missing pumpkins.
Grurg's heard that there's a troll town in the nearby Norwegian mountains and is trying to book on to a tour. Dorian the vampire has noticed a mouth-watering picnic. So long as it's sandwiches he's tempted by, and not somebody's neck...! Can you give them any clues?

NIAGARA FALLS • ONTARIO • CANADA

FRIGHTFUL FALLS

The search isn't over yet!
Harriet's transported the group to the location of one whopping water feature. The spooky squad have touched down in Canada, beside Niagara Falls.

Viola's having a wonderful time wafting around in the water vapour, but Frankie's worried about sliding over on the slippery stones. Hopefully none of the pumpkins have taken a tumble over the top of the falls... See if you can spot all ten!

SHIBUYA CROSSING • TOKYO • JAPAN

FREAKY STREETS
This road crossing in bustling Tokyo is one of the busiest in the world – not the best place to try and find some missing pumpkins! Still, Harriet and the gang are trying their best to spot them.
Dave the skeleton is thriving on all the drama, but Tangle's worried about getting one of their eight feet trodden on. Can you give the monsters a hand to find the ten Tokyo pumpkins?

MONSTERS AT THE MARKET
These floating boats are filled with fresh fruits and vegetables but it's just pumpkins the spooky squad are searching for. Can you find them among the colourful commodities?
There are so many interesting things for Mutt to sniff he doesn't know which way to turn. The monsters had better not draw too much attention to themselves though, or there will be market mayhem!

FLOATING MARKET • MEKONG DELTA • VIETNAM

STATESIDE SEARCH
The group have arrived in Washington D.C., still in pursuit of those pesky pumpkins. How many can you find beneath the massive monument?
Liesel the gargoyle would love to see what the view is like from the top of the tower, even if there are 897 steps! Harriet's getting tired of all the crowds, however. Help her round up the spooky squad by spotting them all in the scene.

WASHINGTON MONUMENT • WASHINGTON D.C. • UNITED STATES

TIVOLI GARDENS • COPENHAGEN • DENMARK

FRIGHT AT THE FUN FAIR

As if the rollercoasters at this world-famous theme park weren't scary enough, now the place has been overrun with monsters and spooks! The gang have appeared in Copenhagen's crowded Tivoli Gardens – a tricky place to play hunt-the-pumpkin.

Tangle and Frankie are trying to get everyone to ride the bumper cars, but Dave's definitely not keen. They look way too wild for him! Who else can you find at the fun fair?

SYDNEY HARBOUR • SYDNEY • AUSTRALIA

HARBOUR HORRORS
The spooky gang have popped up in Sydney Harbour, hoping to find ten more of the missing pumpkins. But where have they got to around this Australian landmark?
Before the monsters whizz off to their next destination, there's just enough time for the group to take a selfie outside Sydney Opera House. See if you can spot the whole gang so they can get a snap together.

SCARY SCOTLAND

There are just ten final pumpkins to track down, and they're hidden somewhere in this Scottish city! Can you find the last of the lost decorations around the cobbled streets of Edinburgh?

Frankie's feeling sad the search is nearly over but Grurg is ready to get back to the dark, dismal corridors of Castle Gloombog. He's had enough adventuring to last him for centuries!

TELEPHONE
TELEPHONE
TELEPHONE
TELEPHONE
TELEPHONE
TELEPHONE
EDINBURGH FESTIVAL FRINGE • EDINBURGH • SCOTLAND

ANSWERS

MENACING VENICE

LOST IN THE LOUVRE

PARK PUMPKINS

SCARE IN THE SQUARE

CREEPY CAUSEWAY

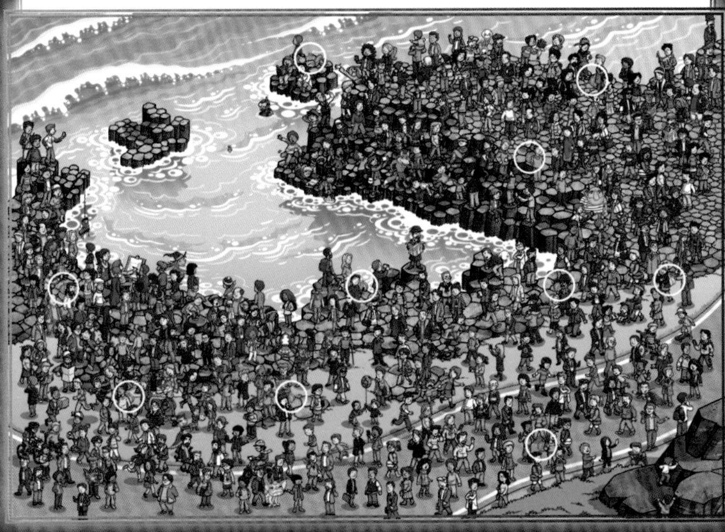

MOUNTAIN MONSTERS

FRIGHTFUL FALLS

FREAKY STREETS

MONSTERS AT THE MARKET

STATESIDE SEARCH

FRIGHT AT THE FUN FAIR

HARBOUR HORRORS

SCARY SCOTLAND

DID YOU FIND THE SPOOKY SQUAD?

There are **nine** characters to find in each scene. Place a tick next to each character after you've found them in every place.

Published in the UK by Scholastic, 2022
1 London Bridge, London, SE1 9BA
Scholastic Ireland, 89E Lagan Road, Dublin Industrial Estate,
Glasnevin, Dublin, D11 HP5F

SCHOLASTIC and associated logos are trademarks and/or
registered trademarks of Scholastic Inc.

Packaged for Scholastic by Plum5 Limited

ISBN 978 0702 31797 2

A CIP catalogue record for this book is available from the British Library.

Printed in China
Paper made from wood grown in sustainable forests and other controlled sources.

1 3 5 7 9 10 8 6 4 2

www.scholastic.co.uk

MIX
Paper from
responsible sources
FSC® C008047

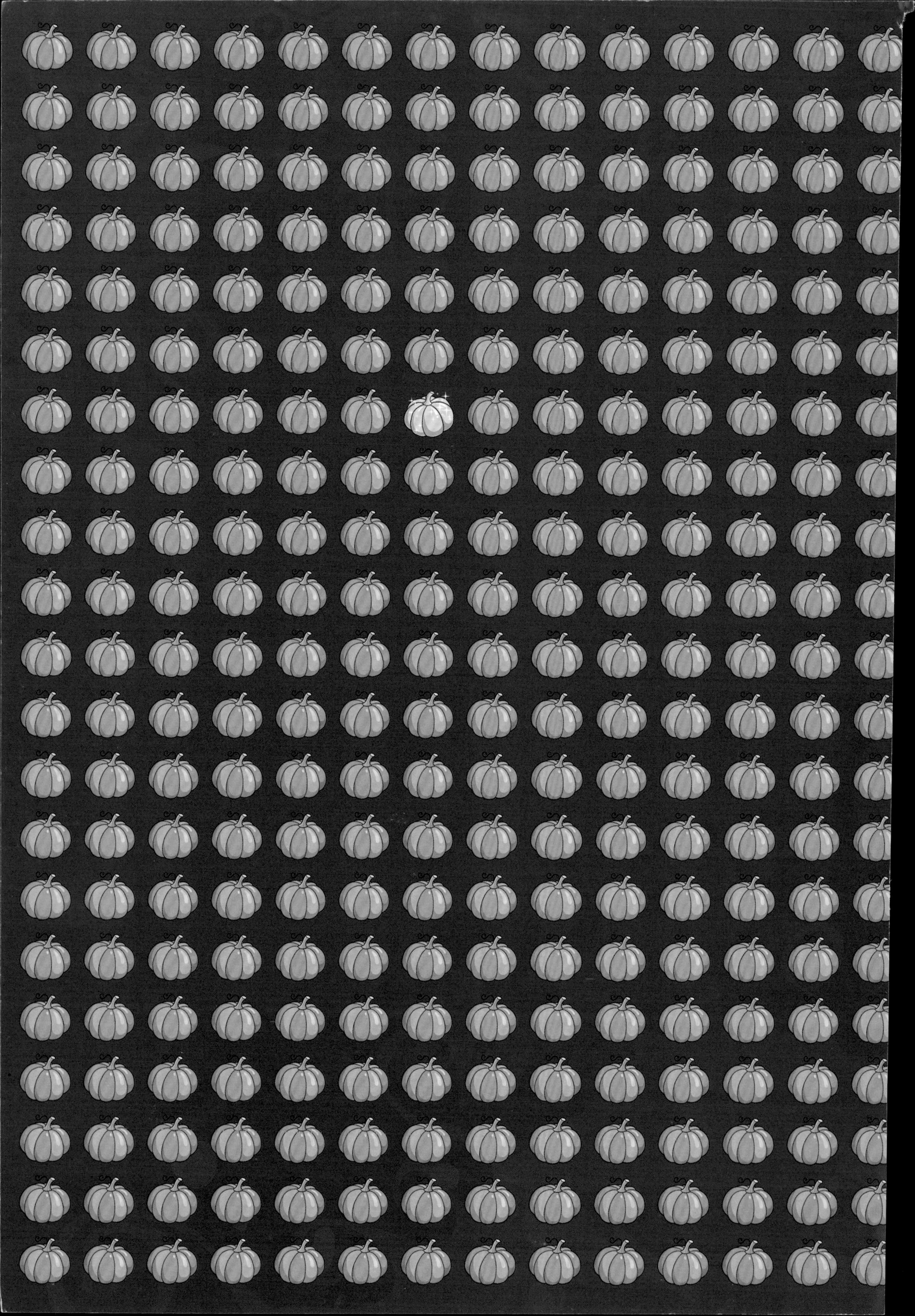